THE MIDNIGHT HOUSE

THE MIDNIGHT HOUSE

Eibhlís Carcione

Illustrated by Beatriz Castro

Collins

Chapter 1

One grey foggy Saturday, Clarabelle Graves was staring through the cracked window of the vintage shop at the doll's house. It wasn't the first foggy Saturday she'd done this. It wasn't just any old doll's house. It was The Midnight House. And now she wanted it so badly her teeth hurt. She wanted it so badly she felt dizzy. She wanted it so badly she couldn't sleep. She wanted it so badly her brain froze, like when she ate too much ice cream.

The shop seemed to appear out of nowhere a few weeks ago, sandwiched between a clothing alterations shop and a charity shop. Clarabelle and her mum went to the charity shop every Saturday morning; they liked to rummage around for bargains or little treasures. Clarabelle had got a hoodie recently and her mum had got a silver teapot that made the best tea. But she'd never seen the vintage shop before.

On that very first morning, she heard a loud squawk on the roof where a raven with shiny wings was perched. It was very like the raven in the oil painting in the vintage shop window. There was no sign up, but the shop had been painted a silvery-grey colour like the moon and had a glossy

black front door with a star-shaped doorknob. There were a few things on display: a music box, a painted vase, a glass case with a stuffed fox, a chipped dinner set with blue flowers and, in the middle of the floor, lots of unopened boxes. A crooked grandfather clock stood in a dusty corner.

She was sure no one was in the shop, until she saw an explosion of dust and heard a clatter that sent her running to her mum who was outside the charity shop next door, chatting to their neighbour, Iris Ryle.

"This is so strange, Mum. How could this shop just appear? I'm sure there was nothing here before," said Clarabelle.

"There are shops opening and closing all the time. I can't keep up either," said her mum. Lydia Graves was a tall woman with chestnut hair; her brown dress and navy fleece were both charity shop finds.

"It looks like a second-hand shop. I must have a look when it opens," said Iris, before heading off with her pull-along shopping trolley.

Clarabelle had forgotten about the new shop until the following Saturday when she saw a black sign with white writing, *The Raven's Nest*, hanging from a rusty chain above the shop door. *What a cool name,* she thought.

As her mum hunted for more bargains next door, Clarabelle took a deep breath and entered the shop. It was now fully stocked with some unusual things like a spinning wheel, wind chimes and a golden chandelier with birds like nightingales. A door creaked and a man stepped from a hidden storeroom carrying a large doll's house.

He held it like it was the most precious object in the world, and he had a faint smile and a look like he was lost in a daydream.

Clarabelle stood for a while, looking at the doll's house. It was black with silver-grey window frames and shutters. It had a carved nameplate in gold above the door which read, *The Midnight House*. Seeing that made her heart drum wildly. There were a few cracks in the walls and a broken slate, but Clarabelle thought it was the most beautiful doll's house ever.

The man dusted it with an orange cloth. He was tall, his hair as dark as the raven, with a few threads of grey. He wore a black tailcoat with silver buttons, a black velvet waistcoat with a silver pocket watch and pinstripe trousers. His clothes were old-fashioned but looked expensive and Clarabelle wondered if she could afford to buy things here.

"Hello," he said, in a cheery, sing-song voice, as he carefully placed the doll's house on display in the front window. "My name's Mr Arnold. I see you've taken a shine to The Midnight House. People think it looks run-down. But I know you see the beauty in it, Clarabelle."

"How do you know my name?" she asked.

"I've heard your mother call you that every

Saturday morning. You know, The Midnight House is unique; houses like this choose their owners. Special, unique people."

Clarabelle wondered if she was special enough to own The Midnight House one day.

"I love that doll's house," she said to her mum outside.

"I think it's seen better days," said her mum, peering through the glass.

"But we can fix it up," Clarabelle told her.

"Look! It costs 100 pounds!" Mum pointed to the price tag hanging from the doorknob.

That was it, thought Clarabelle. She knew she wouldn't be able to get The Midnight House now. But she still looked through the window at it, every Saturday, and wished for it. There was something about it that made her very happy.

Clarabelle couldn't wait to show The Midnight House to her best friend, Tobias. His parents had a family bakery in the city called Abara's, and when Mrs Abara said Clarabelle and Tobias could come along to the bakery and get macaroons, Clarabelle took Tobias on a detour past The Raven's Nest.

"Isn't it beautiful?" she said, catching her breath.

Tobias twisted his mouth. "I think it's about to fall apart. You've never been into dolls before."

"But this one's special," Clarabelle told him. "Just look at the shimmering nameplate."

"The Midnight House." Tobias sighed. "Come on, Clarabelle, let's go to the bookshop. I want

to check out some new graphic novels. Then we can get the macaroons!"

Suddenly, a shadow fell over the doll's house. Tobias jumped back from the window where a man seemed to step from the darkness.

"That's just Mr Arnold. He's the owner," said Clarabelle.

Mr Arnold stopped and flashed a big smile at Clarabelle. He beckoned for them to come

in, but Tobias tugged Clarabelle's sleeve. "Come on, Clarabelle, let's go," he urged.

Clarabelle turned to steal one last look at The Midnight House. Mr Arnold stood in the window, his eyes wide and dark like pools of oil.

"The owner sure seems strange," Tobias mumbled.

"Well, I think he's nice and that house is so cool," said Clarabelle.

Tobias rolled his eyes. Clarabelle felt a jolt of disappointment that her best friend wasn't interested in The Midnight House.

Clarabelle was thinking about the doll's house all that week at school. She felt silly but she couldn't help it. The following Saturday, she raced back to The Raven's Nest; she just had to see The Midnight House. She entered the shop and breathed in a blast of lavender and something as sweet as sherbet.

"I can see you haven't forgotten about The Midnight House, Clarabelle," said Mr Arnold, who was behind the huge old-fashioned till.

"I like it but it's too expensive," whispered Clarabelle.

"Well, I might be able to sell it to you for 70 or even 50 pounds," he told her. "I'll think about it. Because it's important The Midnight House goes to the right person."

Clarabelle didn't know what to say. She began thinking that she might be able to get 50 pounds without asking her mum. She could save her pocket money. She could do odd jobs for her neighbours. Maybe she could even work in The Raven's Nest at weekends.

Chapter 2

Another week went by, and Saturday saw Clarabelle outside The Raven's Nest again, staring at The Midnight House. She couldn't stop thinking about it, especially after Mr Arnold said he might give her a discount. At the same time, she felt bad for wanting it. It was just her and her mum, and they didn't have much money. They were happy together, but sometimes Clarabelle wished she could magically wipe away the worry lines from her mum's forehead.

Her mum was next door in the charity shop. Clarabelle hoped she would be there a while so that she could keep looking at the doll's house, but before she knew it, her mum was back.

"Look at this gorgeous cardigan, Clarabelle. It was only eight pounds."

"That's a bargain, Mum," Clarabelle replied.

"I see you've still got your heart set on the old doll's house," her mum said. "That roof looks ready to collapse."

"It's only a broken slate," Clarabelle pointed out. "Please, Mum, please think about it. It's so beautiful. I won't want a birthday gift for the next three years, if you get me The Midnight House."

Clarabelle loved the gold nameplate above the front door. The only other house she had seen with a nameplate was Nancy Taafe's house – she was one of the most popular girls in her class. There was a silver nameplate over the door which read, *Taafe's Townhouse*.

Nancy's parents were lawyers. Clarabelle had been to some of Nancy's parties. The house made her dizzy with the white carpets, chandeliers and mirrors. Nancy's bedroom was the size of Clarabelle's entire flat; it had a walk-in wardrobe and even an ensuite.

"Never compare," her mum often said, and she tried not to. But sometimes she did, especially on rainy, cold days in the flat.

Clarabelle couldn't stop talking about The Midnight House as they walked back from the market area of the city. She also couldn't stop thinking about where the shop had come from. Pigeons cooed from the rooftops, and one poked its head out of the eaves and winked at Clarabelle as if it knew her secret wish.

As they neared their flat, which was in a grey, boxy building overlooking the river, Thomas Wells, who lived in the basement, passed them. He was wearing his usual dark trench coat and grey, threadbare fingerless gloves. His fingers were blue with speckles of pink. Clarabelle guessed he was on his way to the pigeon-keeper down the street. She often saw him over the wall, the birds perched on his shoulders or flocking at his feet, as he tossed them grains.

"Hello, Lydia and dearest Clarabelle."

That's all he ever said. There were rumours that he was once a professor in a university, but something happened, and he lost everything, and that's how he ended up in number 7, Blackwater Quay.

Sometimes, Clarabelle felt ashamed of the block of flats where she lived. They were built about 20 years ago but now had a greenish tint. The hallway had peeled-off paint and yellow patches of damp.

The stairs were creaky with loose banisters. There was always a smell of must and stale polish. She felt lucky they were on the third floor because there were leaks on the fifth floor. Iris Ryle lived above them on the fourth floor, and she said she had three buckets in different places around her flat. She was still waiting for the landlord, Mr Roycroft, to do something about the leaks.

"Any day now," her mum said to Iris.

But Clarabelle knew Iris would be waiting for months. Clarabelle had met Mr Roycroft a few times, a man in a cream suit with silver hair and a moustache that made him look like a walrus. He did spot checks on the flats. He always complimented her mum on keeping theirs so nice, but Clarabelle felt annoyed by how he was nosing around the flat. It was their home, after all. But her mum reminded her that this was the only flat she could afford and that she would have to keep on the right side of Mr Roycroft.

There were five flats in the building and Clarabelle knew all the tenants. She'd grown up with Thomas Wells and Iris Ryle. Petra Jelinski on the second floor had moved in a few years ago. She was a watercolour artist with long henna-coloured hair and rings on every finger. She knew Clarabelle was interested in art and she would sometimes invite her in to look at her new pieces, which were usually forests and mountains.

Arthur Ledwidge was on the first floor. He was bald with grey, round-rimmed glasses and was so tall he had to bend his head coming in the front door. He was a librarian and a writer. Iris always said he burnt the midnight oil, which meant he stayed up all night writing books, and that's why he had bluish bags under his eyes. Clarabelle and her mum had just received an invitation to his next book launch in the library. She was looking forward to seeing all the neighbours there.

Most of her classmates lived in fancy flats and cosy houses. At least, that's what it seemed like. She wondered how much longer she'd have to live in a run-down flat. But she knew in her heart that this would be her home forever.

Chapter 3

Clarabelle's mum worked long mornings in the kitchen at the local hospital. Clarabelle was born just before her mum was due to start university and study English, so she ended up getting a job. Mum said she'd been happy with Clarabelle's dad, Julian, who was a musician. But when Clarabelle was 18 months old, he left them and moved to Boston. He sent birthday cards and gifts until Clarabelle was five; when she was six, the cards and the gifts stopped and soon he vanished completely from her life.

Clarabelle still had the toy toucan her dad had given her. She'd look at it sometimes and think about him, even if she wasn't sure how she was supposed to be feeling about someone she barely remembered. She had his photo in her drawer and sometimes she'd take it out and look at it. She assumed he was busy with his new life in Boston. Apparently, he played violin in an orchestra; that's why when she heard violin music she thought about him.

Mum still read lots of books. She was a member of an online book club and was always rummaging in second-hand bookshops.

"Please think about The Midnight House, Mum. It could be an early birthday present. I won't ask for any birthday gifts for the next three years if I can have it," Clarabelle said again at dinner, as they ate their spicy chickpea curry and naan bread.

Before her mum could reply, Clarabelle heard Tobias's footsteps on the stairs. He was just in time for their Saturday film tradition.

"Here are some caramel slices and a Nigerian vanilla pound cake," he said, handing her a bag from Abara's bakery.

"Cool," said Clarabelle, breathing in their smell.

She loved the cakes from Tobias's family's bakery. That was one of the things she liked about going to his house; there was always a sweet scent of pastry in the air. She thought he was lucky to have his choice of buns and cakes, but he said he never saw his dad as he worked long hours, so she guessed it wasn't all as perfect as she imagined.

Clarabelle settled on the sofa with a fleecy throw wrapped around her knees, ready to munch popcorn and watch the film with Tobias.

"I have news," Tobias announced.

"Does the news involve a word that starts with R?" Clarabelle guessed.

"Yes! I think Mum and Dad have caved in. We went to the rescue centre and there were two Mini Lop rabbits. I think they're going to get them for my birthday. I'm going to call the white one Snowy and the grey one Hoppy."

"I love the names. This is so exciting!"

Clarabelle crossed her fingers for Tobias. He'd been begging for a dog or a cat for years and nothing had happened, so they were now crossed off his pet list. His new list had a rabbit, a hamster, a bearded dragon or a goldfish, in that order. She hoped he'd get the rabbits.

The film was funny, but Clarabelle couldn't stop thinking about The Midnight House. She pictured her mum handing the money to Mr Arnold. "Your daughter Clarabelle will have many years of happiness with The Midnight House," Mr Arnold would say, as he put it in the back seat of her mum's car. Clarabelle would help her mum put it in her bedroom and then they would celebrate with a cup of tea and some chocolate biscuits.

Tobias looked at her a few times when she didn't laugh. "Are you OK?" he asked.

"Great!" she replied. "This is a fun film."

But Tobias could see she wasn't paying much attention, so after the film finished, he went straight home without really saying goodbye.

She often wished she could be as calm and chilled as Tobias. He was into nature documentaries and their teacher, Ms Chapelle, often gasped at his knowledge of wild animals. He liked graphic novels too and went to karate class on Fridays; he was currently going for his green belt.

Tobias lived in a two-storey townhouse on a busy street. It had a long back garden with swings and decking, and a front garden with a bench and flowerpots. In summer, she and Tobias would always go to the corner shop for ice lollies and sit in Tobias's front garden eating them. Neighbours would say, "Hi, Clarabelle and Tobias", when they went past. Sometimes, she wished those summers wouldn't end, but at least Tobias was in her class.

In winter, Mrs Abara would light the fire and Clarabelle and Tobias would stretch out on the large corner sofa and watch cartoons and films and nibble pretzels. Tobias had got her interested in bird-watching. He said the best place to see birds was from Clarabelle's bedroom window. He told her the names of the different gulls and showed her the little egret and the dipper.

Tobias told her that she was very lucky to live with a view of the river. But how could he say that? The flat's central heating didn't always work; on cold winter days, if she put her hand on the wall,

it would feel like a sheet of ice. She had to wear bed-socks in summer, thick woollen scarves in winter, and every autumn her mum had to set mousetraps, as there were lots of cracks and holes in the walls. One time, her mum had to call Pest Control after she saw a water rat on the kitchen counter.

Clarabelle often thought that if the wind was a musician her flat would be an ideal instrument, as it was full of gaps and holes for the wind to whistle through. Tobias would say nice things about it all the time, like how it was much bigger inside than you'd expect. She knew he was just trying to cheer her up. It was just four rooms: a kitchen/living room, two bedrooms and a bathroom the size of a mouse's cloakroom. Tobias said his cousin in London lived in a bedsit, which was just one room, so maybe he wasn't just trying to be nice about it.

When Clarabelle went to bed that night, she kept moving her pillow around, trying to get comfortable. She was reading a mystery book, but she had to put it down after a few pages. Her eyes were fixed to the corner of the room beside her bed where she would put The Midnight House. It was the perfect spot. She closed her eyes and pictured it, rising from the floor with its silver-grey shutters and its broken slate that made it extra cool. She just knew when she turned on the bedroom light that the nameplate would shine like a shooting star. She crossed her fingers and her toes that she could have it.

Clarabelle often got lonely in her draughty bedroom. Sometimes, she went into a world of make-believe where she imagined she was living with her mum in a beautiful house, and her dad was with them. But that wasn't real.

Mice scuttling in the pipes of the house next door often woke her. She was always afraid a bird or a mouse would fall down the old fireplace, which was boarded up and hidden behind her wardrobe. But there were still plenty of holes and cracks for a mouse or bird to come in.

Clarabelle couldn't stop herself from yawning; her eyes were as heavy as stones. Her bones ached with longing for The Midnight House. She didn't know why she was thinking about it so much.

Chapter 4

On Monday, Clarabelle could only think that she'd have to go through a full week of school before she could look in the window of The Raven's Nest again. One week until she could see The Midnight House.

She was a bit teary-eyed during breakfast. "I really would love The Midnight House, Mum."

"But sometimes we don't get what we wish for."

Her mum reminded her of the orange stray tabby kitten she smuggled into the flat. She knew pets weren't allowed but when Clarabelle had seen the lonely kitten yowling on the doorstep, she couldn't stop herself bringing it in from the cold.

She'd even given it a name – Marmie.

"Mr Roycroft was so angry, I thought he'd kick us out if we hadn't taken the kitten to an animal shelter. And where would we have gone? Rents are too high in the city. We might have ended up in a hostel."

Whenever Clarabelle was out with Tobias and she saw an orange tabby she said, "That could be Marmie."

"There are hundreds of orange tabbies in the city, but I suppose you're right, it could be Marmie," he'd say back.

Clarabelle had a busy week at school. Ms Chapelle was off sick, and they had a supply teacher called Ms Bowe who allowed students to whisper during written work. Clarabelle did lots of interesting stuff like origami and coding, instead of actual schoolwork.

Clarabelle didn't mention The Midnight House to her mum all week. But then she had a terrible dream that Nancy from school got it. Nancy had a collection of porcelain dolls; Clarabelle had been to her house for parties and seen them in a special glass cabinet. A real fear grew in her that Nancy would ask her parents for the doll's house. And of course, they would buy it for her because they knew she loved dolls.

Clarabelle thought about the cracked roof, and she had a feeling Nancy might not like that. But there would be other children shopping with their parents who'd look in the window and see the gold nameplate and want it. Clarabelle told her mum about the dream the next morning.

"I thought Nancy was into horses," Mum replied. "You used to be such good friends."

"I see her in school, Mum. But now Laura Sanchez is friends with her. Things are different. Three's a crowd. And I know Nancy and Laura whisper about me and other kids."

Tobias was her true friend. Other than him, she was friendly with her classmates, but she kept her distance. That made school easier for her. Or at least she thought so.

Clarabelle missed Ms Chapelle, but Ms Bowe kept them busy and that suited her. But soon she couldn't drown out the sweet voice of Mr Arnold in her head. *It will go to only someone very special.*

She was so lost in her daydreams that she was making silly mistakes, and the teacher was now hovering a lot by her desk, which made her make even more mistakes.

On Wednesdays, Clarabelle usually went to Tobias's after school. They did their homework together and Clarabelle stayed for dinner. Sometimes Mrs Abara made fried plantain and spicy jollof rice; Mrs Abara usually gave her a bag of buns to take home, and she and her mum would have some for supper.

At home time, Clarabelle asked Tobias to walk home by The Raven's Nest so they could see The Midnight House.

"I've seen it before," he said.

Clarabelle felt flustered and told him in that case, she would go straight home.

Tobias hunched his shoulders and walked away. He didn't look too pleased, but Clarabelle needed some time to herself. She needed time to think about The Midnight House.

Her mum often went to the café with Iris and Petra on Wednesdays, but cancelled her plans when Clarabelle came home and said she had a headache.

"You never get headaches," she said, feeling her forehead.

"Don't worry, Mum, it's nothing. The class is noisy with the supply teacher."

Clarabelle lay on the sofa, before doing her homework. She'd made up her mind not to mention The Midnight House again. She knew her mum had enough pressure with work and bills.

She remembered one day at school when some of the girls had seen her tights had a rip in them. Laura Sanchez had shaken her head and made a tut-tut sound.

"That's just a small rip," her mum had said, when Clarabelle had come home crying. "And you have a few other pairs."

"But they're ripped too," Clarabelle had said. "Surely we can afford tights. I don't want the other girls staring at me."

Mum said there was a girl in her class when she was at school called Nora who annoyed her. Mum said if she could go back in time, she would have stood up for herself more with Nora. "Stand up for yourself, Clarabelle Graves."

Her mum squeezed her so tight that she still felt it days later. It gave her the strength she needed in the classroom. She could do with a few more of those hugs.

When she asked about The Midnight House again, Clarabelle told her mum, "When you're a child, it's nice that some wishes come true."

Her mum looked at her, with a strange expression. Clarabelle didn't know if it was sadness or anger, or a mix of the two.

Chapter 5

The next day at school, Tobias told Clarabelle he had good lop-eared rabbit news, and he would talk to her at break. But at breaktime, Clarabelle began chatting to him about The Midnight House and he walked away.

On the way out of the school gate, she caught up with him and asked him about the rabbits, but his face reddened.

"You're not interested in my rabbits. All you think about now is that old doll's house."

Clarabelle knew she'd upset him, but all she wanted was for Saturday to come quickly so she could stand outside The Raven's Nest and gaze in at The Midnight House.

She cried a little on the way home, but she wiped her tears. She didn't want her mum to know, or she'd begin to ask questions.

When she got back, Iris was chatting to Thomas Wells in the hallway.

"Are you OK, Clarabelle? Have you been crying?" Iris asked.

"You look very sad," said Thomas.

"I'm fine," Clarabelle said, running up the stairs, almost toppling headfirst into Arthur Ledwidge with his pile of books.

Mum was standing in the kitchen, wearing her apron, and her hands were covered in flour. She'd made pizza dough. Clarabelle eyed the baguette on the counter. Her mum would be making homemade garlic bread too. Clarabelle's appetite was back in an instant. This was exactly what she needed.

"Go and change and I'll put on the kettle. You look a little washed out," Mum said.

Clarabelle went into her room and immediately smelt the scent of candles and lavender. When she looked up, her tummy did cartwheels and backflips all at once.

She couldn't believe it. There it was. The Midnight House was in the corner by her bed, in the exact place she'd imagined it would go.

It wasn't a figment of her imagination any more. It was really there, in front of her, in the corner of her room, placed on the faded brown carpet. Clarabelle approached it carefully and stood beside it. She ran her fingers along the gold nameplate, the shiny black walls, the delicate, silver-grey shutters and the front door with the gold knob that matched the nameplate. It was just perfect. She smiled at the cracked slate on the roof. *There must be some way to open the front of it,* she thought, but there were no hinges or catches. It didn't matter though; now the house was hers, there was plenty of time to work out how to get inside.

Then she peeled her eyes away from it and ran out to her mum. She flung her arms around her.

She was so happy, she couldn't feel her fingers or her toes.

"Mum, I can't believe it. You got me The Midnight House."

"I knew you loved it. I had money put away for a rainy day. Mr Arnold was so nice, he offered it to me for half price. I'll build up the rainy-day kitty again."

This was turning into one of the best days ever. Clarabelle rushed through dinner, hardly tasting the food. She didn't feel like watching TV that evening either. She spent a lot of time running in and out of her room to see The Midnight House, and then rushing to tell her mum what she could see through the windows: the winding staircase, the grandfather clock with its moon face and star-studded hands, and the black velvet sofa. She was almost breathless with happiness.

Clarabelle didn't go straight to bed that night. She wrapped herself in a blanket and sat beside the doll's house. The streetlights shone in through the curtains and washed it with orange light. She brushed her fingers over the nameplate, and it almost seemed to shimmer like when she'd seen it in the window of the shop.

At first, she thought The Midnight House was empty, but as she peered through the windows, she was surprised to see that it wasn't. There were three dolls sitting in the living room next to the huge downstairs window, and they were staring at her. One was a girl with long, dark hair and a blue silk dress. The second doll was a boy in a brown velvet waistcoat and a beige cravat, with dark hair combed to the side. The third was a tall woman in a gold gown and matching bonnet, with dark hair tied in a side plait.

Clarabelle tried to open the front door to reach them, but it wouldn't budge. She didn't want to force it, in case the doorknob fell off. Mr Arnold told her antiques were fragile and had to be handled with care. She peeked in the windows at the shiny furniture, the ornaments and the marble fireplace. If this was a real house, it would be fit for a princess. The bedrooms had four-poster beds with red silk curtains and fluffy, snow-deep carpets.

When she was so tired she couldn't keep her eyes open, Clarabelle smiled and went to bed, all curled up under the duvet. She knew she would sleep better now that she finally had The Midnight House. She wouldn't feel as lonely. This was the kind of house she wished she lived in.

In her dreams, Clarabelle heard strange and wonderful voices. She heard the honey-sweet voice of Mr Arnold from The Raven's Nest. "The Midnight House has found the best home. It could only belong to a special person like Clarabelle Graves."

Then a girl's voice rose over Mr Arnold's, in a sing-song. "Clarabelle, Clarabelle … come here. It's midnight! We so want to meet you. We're so excited."

Clarabelle awoke with a start. Where were the voices coming from? She looked at The Midnight House. The three dolls were still at the window. Then she saw their faces light up, their mouths open and their hands move. They sang:

"Come to the door
And you will meet

The best friends in the world
In this magic house
Of forever midnight."

This was no dream. Clarabelle was suddenly wide awake and sitting up in bed. She was going to turn on the lamp on her bedside locker, but she saw that the lights were already on inside the doll's house. Then she heard tapping. At first it was faint, then it got louder and louder.

Her heart thundered. She crept out of bed and looked at The Midnight House.

She couldn't believe what she was seeing. The dolls were standing close to the window with their hands on the pane, and they were calling for her. "Come here, Clarabelle," they cried.

How did they know her name? She was so afraid, she wanted to run back to bed and pull the duvet over her head. But this was the doll's house she'd wanted for so long; part of her was excited and curious, it was so magical, so she found herself on her knees at the front door. The gold nameplate burnt brightly like the midsummer sun.

She turned the knob of the front door, and it opened this time.

"Clarabelle is here," a voice said sweetly.

She felt soft hands clutch hers and pull her gently. Her body seemed to float for a few seconds and swirl in empty space; then everything went dark, and in a flash, she found herself in a room with a large table covered by a red-rose tablecloth and five chairs with red leather seats. In front of her was a dresser with china tea sets and ornaments. In one corner of the room, there was a winding staircase. In the other corner, there was a large black velvet sofa and two rocking chairs beside a blazing log fire. It looked like a perfect place to curl up with a book or watch TV.

Everywhere she looked there were candles burning. She was inside the doll's house!

The girl doll rushed over to Clarabelle and gave her a hug. The boy doll and the lady doll both clapped with glee. Their eyes were oval like blue pearl drops, and their lips were pink like hyacinths.

"Welcome, Clarabelle," they said. "Welcome to The Midnight House."

Chapter 6

Clarabelle pinched her wrists to make sure this was real. She felt the pinch but wondered if she was pinching her wrists in the dream. But no, she felt the pinch, and it was a sharp one.

This was really happening. The girl was still hugging her, and Clarabelle felt the doll's cheek against hers. She was real!

"Yes, we're real. We're alive, Clarabelle," said the doll, as if she could read her mind. She did a curtsey and twirled around Clarabelle like a ballerina in her gold satin shoes. "This is our parlour. My name is Evie, and this is my brother, Merlin."

"Welcome, my dearest Clarabelle," he said, with

a firm handshake.

Clarabelle thought he looked smart in his cravat and waistcoat.

The whistle of a kettle made her turn. It was at that moment she laid eyes on the mother doll; she looked like a good queen in a fairy tale. Clarabelle stepped towards her and shook her hand. It was smooth like expensive wrapping paper, but ice-cold.

"I'm Clarice. Welcome to The Midnight House. We've been waiting for you, special girl. Join us for tea and cake," she said, in a sweet sing-song voice.

Clarabelle sat at the table with the three dolls. They were living, breathing people. She couldn't believe what she was seeing and couldn't believe where she was.

Clarice poured the tea into china teacups. Clarabelle brought the cup to her mouth, still in a daydream, and sipped the tea and ate a chocolate bun. The tea was warm and the chocolate bun was so sweet it melted on her tongue.

The dolls ate too, but their eyes were always on Clarabelle.

Clarabelle had never been in a house this warm; she could feel the candles burning all around the room. She'd also never been in a house as beautiful as this. It was the strangest experience. One minute, she felt so afraid she wanted to break down the door of The Midnight House and hide in bed. The next moment, she wished her visit would never end. She felt she belonged with Evie, Merlin and Clarice.

The dolls quizzed her about her favourite food.

"I love my mum's homemade pizza," she said.

"Pizza? What's that?" asked Merlin.

Clarabelle described what it was. "My friend likes it too."

"What's your friend's name?" asked Evie.

"Tobias. We're in the same class." At least, Clarabelle thought, he *was* her friend.

"That's nice," said Evie. "But we're your friends now and we'll always be here for you." Evie took a sparkling glass ball from a deep pocket in her dress. "This is a gift for you, Clarabelle. The Midnight House snow globe," she said.

Clarabelle took it in her trembling hands. "It's beautiful."

It felt heavy in her hand, but it was warm and smooth and made her skin tingle. She shook it and watched the snowflakes flutter and dance around The Midnight House. It was almost hypnotic.

"Keep it with you at all times," said Evie. "We'll always be with you when you have it. You mustn't tell anyone about us or The Midnight House or the snow globe. If you do, this magic will break."

Chapter 7

In a blink, Clarabelle was back in her bedroom. The lights were off in the doll's house and the dolls were in their spot at the window. She wondered if she'd imagined the whole thing, but she still had the snow globe in her hand. Clarabelle gave it another shake and watched the snowflakes fall on the roof and windowsills of The Midnight House. It hadn't been a dream. Her heart soared as high as the sky with happiness. She wrapped the globe in one of her scarves and placed it under her pillow.

Mum always told Clarabelle not to keep secrets. But Clarabelle knew that if she told Mum The Midnight House was magical, she wouldn't believe her, and the dolls had told her not to say anything or the spell would break. If Mum found out, she might get rid of The Midnight House. Clarabelle wouldn't let this happen!

Clarabelle would have to be careful at school, too. She would keep the snow globe in the side pouch of her bag, wrapped up tightly in the scarf. She climbed into bed and closed her eyes. She lay on her back, she lay on her side, she curled up like a little cat. She couldn't sleep a wink. Evie's words about the snow globe rang in her head. *We'll always be with you when you have it. Keep it with you at all times.*

"I can't believe you forgot it," said Mum, buttering her toast. "I hope The Midnight House hasn't cast a spell on you."

Clarabelle often thought her mum could read her thoughts. She glanced up at the polar bear kitchen calendar. There was a purple ring around the 23rd. Today was Tobias's birthday. She knew his birthday was coming up, but with everything that had happened with The Midnight House, she'd completely forgotten it.

"I have time, Mum. I'll make a card now. And I've got enough money to get the graphic novel he likes at the weekend."

"It's the thought that counts," Mum said.

Clarabelle found some paper; a homemade card was better than a shop card. She drew a grey heron on the front and wrote "Happy Birthday" and "Sorry for being late with the gift". She also added "Sorry for not seeing you much".

When she got to school, she gave Tobias the card. He said thanks, but when he didn't say anything

else, Clarabelle asked him about his birthday party. Tobias usually had lots of family around for his birthday, and Clarabelle was always included. She'd been at all his birthdays since they were six. His mum usually made a three-tier chocolate cake, and they watched a film.

"It's at six," Tobias told her. "But you don't have to come if you're too busy."

"I'll be there. I always come." She wanted to tell him about Evie and Merlin and about what happened at midnight. But then she remembered

what the dolls said. Clarabelle hoped she might convince the dolls to let her tell Tobias and Mum about them, but she would keep quiet until then.

During class, Clarabelle couldn't stop thinking about her next visit to The Midnight House.

"You're a bit of a daydreamer, Clarabelle Graves," Ms Bowe said.

Tobias wasn't very talkative at school. At breaktime, Clarabelle heard some of her classmates talking about the two rabbits he got for his birthday. Usually, she'd be the first to know about her friend's news, but not now.

After school, Clarabelle wanted to walk home with Tobias, but he was nowhere to be seen. She couldn't stop the tears. She'd listened to him talking about wanting a pet for years. And now that he had rabbits, he hadn't even told her. She wiped her eyes. She didn't want her mum to see her upset. She *would* go to his party later and try to act normal.

Chapter 8

As soon as Clarabelle opened the door of the flat, she was hit with the scent of burning candles and lavender again. She wondered if her mum could smell it too.

When Clarabelle entered her bedroom, she couldn't believe her eyes. Evie and Merlin were now the same size as her! They were perched on her bed, smiling. When they asked her where the snow globe was, Clarabelle pointed to the pouch in her bag.

"That's good," said Merlin.

"How did you get here?" asked Clarabelle.

"Sometimes the magic of The Midnight

House lets us out," Evie said.

Clarabelle's heart was beating in her chest. She was so pleased to see them, but she felt like a trapped pigeon in an attic. What would her mum say if she saw the two dolls? She also didn't like the way they were looking around her room. The furniture was second-hand. The walls were damp and that made the primrose-yellow paint bubbly.

Merlin sauntered over to the window and

wrinkled his nose. "The river is filthy and there's a terrible stench. How can you sleep in this room, Clarabelle?" he said. "The seagulls are smelly. There are no ducks or kingfishers. I would hate to live in a flat like this."

Clarabelle felt like crying. They were inspecting everything and seemed to be judging her.

"I'm sorry," Merlin said, when he turned to look

at her. "I didn't mean it. I'm used to the comfort and luxury of The Midnight House. Forget what I said. But I'm your friend and I worry about you."

"Never mind him," Evie said. "He always says what he thinks. But he's right about the flat. It's dingy and poky. The curtains are cheap and the bed is too small. There are holes in the floor and walls. I'm sure it's mouse-infested too."

"Your clothes are odd as well," said Merlin. His smile slithered across his face.

"This is a school uniform," Clarabelle said.

"We're lucky our mother teaches us," Merlin said. "We would hate to wear those clothes. The jumper looks itchy."

Evie opened the wardrobe and furrowed her brow. "I'm going to ask Mama to make you some new clothes," said Evie. "These dresses and coats are moth-eaten and tatty."

"I have plenty of clothes," Clarabelle argued. Tobias would never talk like this about her clothes or her room.

"You deserve pretty clothes," Evie told her. "There are holes in your tights."

"Mum hasn't got a lot of money, but we're happy," Clarabelle argued.

"Your mother must be wonderful because you're wonderful," said Evie. "But I'm upset you live in a grotty flat. It's cold here. I hope you don't become ill."

"We just worry about you," said Merlin.

They'd been so nice to her when they were inside The Midnight House, but now they sounded like some of her classmates, and she didn't like what they were saying. This was her home. It was cold and it was far from perfect, but deep down she still loved it. The more they criticised it, the more Clarabelle realised this: it was her safe place with Mum.

Clarabelle tried to slow her thumping heart. The dolls had come out of the house this time. What next? They'd stepped into her home without even a whisper or a knock. Clarabelle wondered if Clarice was in her room too, lurking in the shadows or hiding in the wardrobe.

Before Clarabelle could ask about Clarice, Evie said: "Oh, Mama is making a special dinner for you. We're all excited about your visit later. Please wear your favourite dress."

Clarabelle felt a little better then. Her favourite dress had red flowers on it. She might also wear her silver, sparkly tights. Suddenly, all she wanted to do was to return to The Midnight House.

Merlin suddenly snatched her sketchbook from her bedside locker and started flicking through the pages. "I think you're a good artist. I'm not sure about some of these pictures though. The old man feeding the pigeons makes me sad. This red-haired woman with all the rings looks strange, and this old woman with the trolley has a strange hairstyle."

Clarabelle blushed and gritted her teeth. "These people are my neighbours and friends."

Merlin smirked. "They look so odd. They're not worth sketching."

"She's a gifted artist," Evie said. "I'm sure you'll be an artist when you grow up, Clarabelle. How exciting!"

Clarabelle did want to be an artist when she grew up, but she also thought she would like to work with people. She loved to spend time with the other tenants. She often saw Iris on Sundays for tea and biscuits and a chat. Sometimes, she went to the art shop with Petra and helped her pick out colours. Suddenly, Clarabelle remembered Tobias's birthday. "I have to go now," she said.

"Why?" asked Evie. "We want to talk to you for longer. We miss you when you're at school."

"I have to see my friend Tobias. It's his birthday."

"But we're your *best* friends."

Clarabelle thought this was a strange thing to say, considering she'd only just met them.

"What's his address?" Merlin said, his eyes glinting like chips of blue glass.

"Why do you want to know?" Clarabelle asked.

Merlin just stared and put his hands on his hips.

"Number 3, Crabbe Lane," Clarabelle said. "I have to go."

"Have a lovely time," said Evie. "We won't delay you because we have to get back to The Midnight House; we can't stay away from the house for too long. But we missed you and we wanted to see you."

Clarabelle saw crinkly lines of sadness etched on Evie's forehead.

They hugged her gently and shrunk down, disappearing behind the door of The Midnight House.

Clarabelle felt as though she'd spent at least an hour talking to the dolls, but according to the clock only five minutes had passed. She was still in time for Tobias's party!

She said goodbye to her mum and ran all the way to his house. She really wanted to tell Tobias about what had happened, but he might tell his parents, and they might contact her mum. That would be a disaster, so in the end, she decided to say nothing.

When she was almost at Tobias's house, she stopped in her tracks. The snow globe felt heavy in her pocket. Her head became fizzy and light, like she had a fever, and suddenly she couldn't face the party. She'd see Tobias the next day at school; she was sure he'd understand.

Clarabelle began walking home. Out of the corner of her eye, she saw a man dressed like Mr Arnold, but he wore a black top hat and used a crimson cane. It was suddenly getting cloudy, and the man turned his head to glance at her.

Clarabelle was going to wave, she was sure it was Mr Arnold, but he walked quickly and disappeared into a crowd.

Clarabelle decided she'd go back to The Raven's Nest at the weekend and ask Mr Arnold about The Midnight House and its magic. He was the man who sold them The Midnight House. He must be the one who knew its secrets.

Chapter 9

That evening Clarabelle set her alarm clock for 20 minutes to midnight. She put on her red floral dress, her matching red leather shoes and her silver, sparkly tights. She looked at her reflection in the wardrobe mirror. She brushed her hair and smoothed her dress.

She knocked lightly on the door of the doll's house and was soon whisked inside by Evie. A familiar aroma wafted through The Midnight House.

"Welcome, dear Clarabelle," said Clarice. "I made your favourite dinner. You're just in time for pizza and garlic bread."

"Thank you," Clarabelle stuttered.

"You look beautiful in your dress," gasped Evie. Evie's hair was in plaits and tied with red ribbons.

Merlin's hair was combed neatly to the side and was glossy like black paint. He offered her lemonade; Clarabelle thought everything was so fancy and decorative. The glasses were gold-tinted, and the napkins were folded into bird shapes.

Clarabelle gasped as she saw the food laid out on the table.

"Papa found the recipe in an old magazine," Evie told her. "We had no idea what pizza was."

They sat down to eat and Clarabelle carefully brought a slice of pizza to her mouth with trembling hands. It certainly smelt like pizza. She took a small bite and smiled. This one was almost as good as her mum's.

Clarice stopped eating. She rested her chin in her hand and smiled at Clarabelle. "I'm so happy you like my cooking."

"It's scrumptious," said Clarabelle. She was

starting to sound like Evie and Merlin.

Clarice smiled and her cheeks turned a deeper cherry-red.

"I think I prefer Mama's liver and onions," observed Merlin.

Evie looked at Clarabelle and they erupted in laughter.

Evie took another nibble of pizza, her eyes locked on Clarabelle all the time. "Sometimes we peep out of the window at you," she said.

Clarabelle dropped her pizza and felt her toes turn to jelly.

"But only when you're asleep," said Evie. "Your room is cold. It makes me sad that you live in a cold flat by the river."

"But it's my home and I like it the way it is," Clarabelle surprised herself by saying.

"Of course you do," said Clarice. "We just get concerned about you."

"I suppose if you didn't live in that flat in the city you would never have gone into The Raven's Nest and you would never have seen The Midnight House," said Merlin. "Your mum would never have bought it, and we would never have met you."

"And now we're all friends," said Evie. She blinked a lot as she spoke; Clarabelle hadn't noticed how long her eyelashes were until now. They looked like they were made from strips of cloth.

Merlin clicked his fingers and made the sound of grasshoppers.

"You're like one of the family," said Clarice. "Make yourself at home. You must keep coming to The Midnight House because we have lots of treats and surprises for you."

Clarabelle wondered when she would meet Papa. She thought it was strange that he hadn't joined them by the fire or for dinner. She wondered where he was and what he was doing.

After dinner, Clarabelle stood at the window with the white silk curtains. She was curious to peer at her bedroom like the dolls did. But before she knew it, Evie and Merlin linked her arms and pulled her to the other window with the black velvet curtains.

"Hey, presto!" said Merlin, throwing back the curtains.

Clarabelle caught her breath. She thought she would see her bedroom, but instead she saw a vast night sky with a bright moon and millions of twinkling stars. The night sky seemed very close, a fingertip away. Merlin had a little pocketbook called *The Night Sky* in his hands, and he was scanning the sky.

"Look at that silver ribbon across the sky. Over there, Clarabelle. That's the Milky Way."

"That's beautiful," said Clarabelle.

"Merlin's a great astronomer," smiled Clarice. "The night sky brings a lot of magic into The Midnight House: the magic of the moon, the stars and the comets."

Clarabelle didn't understand what Clarice meant, but she kept her eyes on the sparkling sky; it was impossible not to watch it, she felt mesmerised by the view.

Merlin pointed to a patch of purplish-red light and said it was the Orion Nebula. Evie nudged her and tapped her finger where Jupiter and Mars shone.

"Where is The Midnight House snow globe?" asked Merlin.

"It's here in my pocket," replied Clarabelle, slowly tapping her dress to feel the globe.

"That's good," said Evie. "Remember, you must always keep it with you so the magic can continue. Don't forget, you're forbidden to tell anyone about it."

"Mum doesn't like me keeping secrets," Clarabelle mumbled, almost to herself.

"I don't like Evie and Merlin keeping secrets either," said Clarice. "But The Midnight House and the snow globe are an exception."

Clarabelle nodded but she felt uncomfortable. She didn't want the magic to be broken, but something didn't feel right.

Suddenly, she felt clammy and thought about her mum in the house all alone. She ran to the window with the white silk curtains again and gazed at her bedroom. A shivery tingle whispered down her back. The bedroom was blurry and looked as far away as the moon and the stars.

"Be careful, dear Clarabelle. Sometimes your eyes see things that aren't there," said Evie.

"Your bed is just there beside The Midnight House. What do you see?" asked Clarice.

"I see my bedroom," whispered Clarabelle. "But it's so very far away."

Clarabelle heard sounds coming from upstairs. Creaking sounds, tapping, footsteps, hushed voices. Things were getting stranger and stranger. When Clarabelle mentioned the noise, Evie and Merlin gave her puzzled looks and said she was hearing things.

Suddenly, Clarabelle heard heavy footfalls upstairs, from inside the doll's house, and a door slam like thunder. Evie grabbed Merlin's hand and Clarice cleared her throat.

"Ah, it's late, dear Clarabelle. An hour has passed. I'm sure you'll be staying with us for much longer very soon. We'll see you tomorrow."

"No, Mama! Please can she stay longer?" said Evie.

"They're very fond of you," Clarice said. "They get very lonely here."

"I get lonely too," Clarabelle said, thinking about Tobias. She couldn't even remember why they weren't talking any more.

"That's why real friends are so important," said Merlin. "Someone who has friends is never lonely."

"And family," said Clarabelle. "My mum is family."

"Of course," said Evie, with a curtsey.

Clarice opened the front door. She pushed Clarabelle lightly with hands as cold as winter snowflakes, and she was soon standing in her bedroom at number 7, Blackwater Quay.

Chapter 10

From then on, every night at midnight, Clarabelle entered The Midnight House. Sometimes Clarabelle felt tired in the mornings, but every night The Midnight House tempted her back.

Clarabelle knew she was making lots of mistakes in her schoolwork. She was yawning all the time. Her midnight visits were wearing her out. She was getting low marks in tests and her schoolbag was in chaos. One day, she did her History work in her English book and Ms Chapelle gave her a frosty look.

The more Clarabelle visited The Midnight House, the more she thought Evie and Merlin were the best friends in the world and that Clarice was the kindest mother. She became even quieter and didn't feel like much company. She walked around the schoolyard on her own. Her meals had no taste, because food was far better in The Midnight House. Sometimes, she felt her head was spinning, like she'd spent hours on a wild rollercoaster ride.

"You haven't been reading or watching much TV," her mum said, one evening.

"Of course I have," she replied. Clarabelle now had an answer for everything.

She tried to count the number of times she'd visited The Midnight House, but she couldn't. Everything was becoming foggy. Soon Clarabelle didn't have to wait until midnight to visit the dolls; the moment she got home from school she was pulled into The Midnight House. Evie and Merlin always made her feel welcome, and told her great stories about toymakers who made magical toys in a country where it always snowed.

Evie had sharp hearing, so she would let Clarabelle know when she needed to hurry back to her room.

"I think your mama is on the way," she would say. "Don't worry, Clarabelle. We promise we'll always have you out in time."

Clarabelle would hear the voices when she was asleep, and sometimes when she was awake too, *Clarabelle, sweet Clarabelle, dear Clarabelle* … She knew she was keeping secrets, but she kept lying.

One night, Clarabelle was in The Midnight House, and Merlin and Evie brought her upstairs for the first time. Clarabelle stopped to look at a large oil painting of The Midnight House that seemed to float in mid-air on the wall. In the painting, there were three shadows in the downstairs window. Two of them looked like Evie and Merlin. She didn't know who the other figure was, but she was certain it wasn't Clarice.

"Who's the other doll?" she asked Evie, but Evie's face was blank.

"Maybe it's you, Clarabelle Graves," said Merlin,

sticking his finger inside his cheek and making a popping sound.

"Me? How could I be there?"

"Never mind, Merlin. He's being silly. Let's explore upstairs," said Evie.

The bathroom was huge, with silver tiles, decorated with gold ducks. Evie pulled open the cupboard to reveal hundreds of old-fashioned glass bottles of shampoo and bubble bath.

"We love bubble baths here. Once Merlin had a bubble bath and the bubbles filled the house. So, if you see bubbles coming out of the door into your bedroom, you'll know what's going on in here."

Clarabelle burst out laughing and the two dolls joined in.

"Come on. Wait until you see our bedroom," Evie said, skipping ahead along the endless corridor.

The room took her breath away. It had three four-poster beds with red silk curtains and the finest, velvet wallpaper with painted parrots and flamingos.

"You can lie in the middle bed, Clarabelle," said Evie. "You must stay overnight very soon, and Mama will make us crumpets for breakfast."

"Yes. That would be perfect," said Merlin. "Papa said he's getting a TV and we're going to have a cinema room. Isn't that exciting, dear Clarabelle?"

"Very," said Clarabelle. "But where is your papa?"

"You'll meet him soon," said Evie. "Aren't you going to see how comfy the bed is?"

Clarabelle nestled down deep in the bed. It was so soft like it was made from a million silk feathers. She could sleep here for days and months. It was so comfy, she felt herself nodding off.

She stretched and put her hand on the wallpaper above the bed. It was velvety and warm. She'd love to have a bedroom like this. She still hoped the dolls would bring lots of magic and even riches into her life. She didn't know the day or the hour, but she was sure it would happen. She imagined herself and her mum living in a brand-new townhouse. She'd have a bedroom as big as Evie and Merlin's. The Midnight House would sit in the corner of her new bedroom. Tobias would see it when he came over, but she wouldn't tell him it was magical, in case the magic broke and the dolls wouldn't come alive again.

Clarabelle noticed there was no wardrobe in their bedroom. Evie had looked in her wardrobe and said her clothes weren't nice. But where were their clothes? "Where do you keep your clothes?" she asked.

"In a wardrobe, of course," said Evie. "We have a special dressing room for that. I have lots of beautiful clothes in my wardrobe. But you must see our favourite toys before you go. Our parents get us the most splendid things."

They ushered her into a room with three enormous rocking horses.

"These are the most beautiful rocking horses in the world, and they belong to The Midnight House," said Evie. "Our parents bought them from a world-famous toymaker in a faraway country."

They were nearly the same size as real horses, with silky manes and tails, glittering eyes and carved tongues. Clarabelle gazed in wonder and awe at their muscles and their shiny hooves, the red rosettes in their bridles, the diamonds in their saddles.

"Let me introduce you to the rocking horses," said Merlin, in a loud voice, like a circus ringmaster.

"This magnificent dappled grey horse is called Claudius. This majestic black horse is called Nero, and this spectacular brown horse is called Caesar."

Clarabelle remembered a rocking horse she'd had when she was small. She loved rocking on it but one day, when she sat on it, it broke. Her mum said it was a sign she'd outgrown it. There'd be other toys, Mum said. Clarabelle could never have imagined rocking horses like this existed.

"Let's go to the greatest carnival in the world," said Merlin, mounting Caesar's jewel-studded saddle.

"Come on, Clarabelle," said Evie, springing up on Nero. "Let's have more magical times in this world of forever midnight. But you must close your eyes. We must all hold the reins and close our eyes."

Clarabelle climbed up on Claudius and ruffled his mane. She held the reins and shut her eyes tightly. She thought she heard him whinny and snort, his hooves clip-clopping in the night.

"Off we go to the greatest carnival in the world with Clarabelle Graves," whispered Evie.

Soon Clarabelle was rocking back and forth on Claudius. She heard music in the distance. The tighter she held the reins, the louder the music became. It sounded like merry-go-round music. The air was sweet with candyfloss and candied apples. Clarabelle felt like she went round and round thousands of times. She heard a chorus of whoops and applause from an unseen audience.

Merlin and Evie laughed and laughed.

Then the music became quieter and quieter. The horses began to rock slowly and then became deathly still.

"Come on, Clarabelle," said Evie. "Now we want to show you our parents' room." They all tramped up another staircase into a large room with a sleigh bed and four chandeliers.

Clarabelle's head swam with a hundred thoughts. She wondered about their papa again, but she didn't want to ask more questions. Maybe he was living in a different country like her own dad, and they'd become sad if she asked.

The wallpaper was black with luminous moons and galaxies.

"Isn't it wonderful, dear Clarabelle," said Evie. "Mama and Papa are so lucky. They say it's like sleeping outdoors under the sky. They say they sometimes feel the starlit wind blowing; that's the most magical wind."

Clarabelle thought for a moment. Could the starlit wind bring good luck and happiness into her life? Could it blow away her mother's worries? She spotted two pairs of polar bear slippers under the bed.

"Mama and Papa love those. They said they're going to get us a pair," said Evie. "I'll ask them to get you some too. Isn't your birthday on the 3rd of November?"

How did they know that? Clarabelle thought. She tried to slow her pounding heart, by taking deep, steady breaths. Merlin and Evie pulled her out of the room, and they wandered down more endless, lavender-scented corridors. Soon, they stepped into a room with candy cane wallpaper and painted blue floors, with 30 small beds where dolls were sitting or sleeping under patchwork quilts.

Clarabelle gasped. "That doll looks like me," she said.

"It's got hair like you and the same eyes and the same shaped face," said Merlin, "but it's not you. You're here."

But Clarabelle thought the doll was identical to her. A creeping dread settled on the back of her neck.

"Sometimes we think you see things that aren't

there, dear Clarabelle," said Evie, laughing.

Clarabelle gazed at the doll and was reminded of a photo, taken when she was about six. She was dressed in the same blue dress and cream cardigan. She put her hand on the doll's cheek. Its skin felt warm. She touched the hair, and it felt real. Suddenly, the doll blinked.

Clarice rapped on the door and said it was getting late. Evie and Merlin's faces flushed red with anger. Clarabelle and the two dolls followed Clarice down the winding stairs.

Clarabelle bolted to the window with the white silk curtains and stared out. Her bedroom was spinning further and further away; it looked like it was at the end of a very dark street. She bit back a scream.

"My bedroom looks so far away," she told them.

"It's getting late, dear Clarabelle," said Clarice. "Don't look out of the window again; you're just tired. You need to go now and have a good sleep."

By the time Clarabelle climbed into her own bed, her head was throbbing. She realised she hadn't finished all her homework again. Ms Chapelle said she would have to talk to her mum soon if her work didn't improve. She was living a double life, a life her mum knew nothing about.

Carrying the snow globe everywhere with her was also tiring. What would happen if she lost it? What if her mum found it? What if one of her classmates found it in her schoolbag?

As the weeks went by, Clarabelle spent more and more time in The Midnight House. Sometimes, she didn't want to leave the house at all. But she also noticed that it was taking her longer and longer to get out of the doll's house. And each time she returned to her bedroom, it felt colder and colder.

Chapter 11

Rain lashed the windows of Clarabelle's room, and a harrowing wind moaned in the gaps in the walls. The Midnight House was lit up and she couldn't wait to sit by the fire. There was something different about the doll's house – there was a fourth doll at the landing window. He was dressed in a black tailcoat and a top hat. *Wait,* she thought. *A fourth doll? Was that Evie and Merlin's papa? He wasn't there before.* She was sure of it.

Clarabelle made up her mind to tell the dolls about her worries. She wanted to ask if they could use their magic to help her mum. But she also wanted to tell them that she was falling behind at school, and that Tobias wasn't her friend any more.

But just as the clock struck midnight, she realised the people she needed to talk to *were* her mum and Tobias. The dolls were getting stranger and stranger. For the first time in a while, she wanted to stay in bed and pull the covers over her head. But as soon as she heard the dolls' voices, she found herself walking to the door and entering The Midnight House as usual.

Evie and Merlin greeted her with chuckles and hugs. The fire was lit. Clarice rocked on her rocking chair. The other rocking chair was moving, although there was no one sitting on it. All the dolls' faces were rosy red from the firelight. The table was set with plates and cutlery but there was no sign of food.

Evie's hair was loose, and she wore a tiara with glittering rubies. Clarabelle noticed she had a different look in her eyes; they were blue like the river on a winter's day. Merlin's hair was even glossier, like someone had spilt ink over it.

The grandfather clock with the moon face was ticking and Clarice kept turning her head to peer at it. The hands weren't moving but the ticking was getting so loud, Clarabelle covered her ears.

"Stop that! The clock makes no sound," said Merlin. He puffed out his chest and scowled at her.

Clarabelle flew to the window with the white silk curtains. This time she couldn't see her bedroom at all! It was all a blur. Then she saw something moving. She hoped it was her mum. She began to tremble.

"You silly girl, Clarabelle Graves," Evie said, in a clipped tone. "We told you not to look out of that window."

The dolls looked different tonight, somehow. Their lips were dusky-blue. Rays of moonlight dripped through the windows, shedding a white light on their faces and hands. Clarice's bonnet was on the floor and her long black ringlets slithered like snakes down her back.

"Sit down beside me," said Evie. She squeezed Clarabelle's arm a little tighter than usual and Clarabelle had no choice but to sit between Evie and Merlin on the velvet sofa.

Clarice rocked faster on the rocking chair, gazing into the flames.

Then Clarabelle heard footsteps, heavy footsteps. They were coming down the stairs. She heard a gravelly voice, a familiar voice. It sounded like a man.

"Is that your papa?" Clarabelle asked.

"Yes," said Evie. "He's finally ready to meet you."

"Hello, everyone. I'm so pleased to see Clarabelle here."

The voice made her almost leap out of her skin. The shadow of a tall man in a top hat fell on the stairs.

The fourth doll.

Through the banisters, Clarabelle glimpsed pointed leather shoes, grey pinstripe trousers and the tails of a black coat. But it wasn't a doll at all. It was Mr Arnold, and he smiled at Clarabelle with crystal-white teeth. His cheeks had a red glow like the other dolls. She hadn't noticed that when she met him in the vintage shop.

Clarabelle felt the blood drain from her face. What was Mr Arnold doing in The Midnight House? She looked around at the other dolls as if looking for answers. Their eyes were as bright as the stars.

"Calm down, dear Clarabelle. It's just me," said Mr Arnold. "There's nothing to be afraid of. I told you The Midnight House was special. You know my family, my wife, the lovely Mrs Arnold, and our children, Evie and Merlin." Mr Arnold took a seat opposite Clarice.

The antique pocket watch flashed in his waistcoat. His raven-dark hair turned frosty-grey in the moonlight that was spilling through the parlour window.

Clarabelle couldn't move. Her words died in her throat. How could Mr Arnold be here? Evie and Merlin clutched her hands as Mr Arnold spoke. She listened to every word and every word was like fireworks exploding.

"I know Merlin and Evie have told you stories about the great toymakers in the land where it always snows. I was an apprentice to one of those toymakers," he said, standing up from the chair and taking a bow. "This man wasn't just a toymaker, he was also a wizard. He taught me all his secrets. I made many dolls through the years, but I was very lonely. So, I used all the magic I learnt from the wizard toymaker to make The Midnight House and my family of dolls. I wanted it so badly, just like you wanted The Midnight House so badly. It was this that drew us together."

He paused and cleared his throat. "And you, Clarabelle, are the missing piece."

Merlin and Evie clapped their hands. "Yes! Clarabelle," they squeaked.

"My children were lonely for a friend until we found you. Your doll is waiting upstairs to become you. We tried other children, and they didn't work out. Merlin and Evie got bored with them, so they remain sleeping dolls upstairs. We know you're special. You are the one. Your doll is just as beautiful as you. We want you to stay with us. I promise you a life of forever happiness in The Midnight House."

A wave of ice ran across Clarabelle's skin. She exhaled slowly. "I have my mum. I have Tobias," whispered Clarabelle. "I can't stay here *forever*. I want to see my mum."

"Your mum will get on fine without you," said Evie. "You need us, dear Clarabelle. We're your friends and we need you."

Clarabelle got up and began to walk towards the door. Evie, Merlin and Clarice began to skip around her in a circle. Every footstep and every doll's breath sounded ten times louder than before. She put her hand on her heart to try and soothe it. The dolls started to chant her name over and over again. Clarabelle closed her eyes and moved her hands over her ears, but she still heard them calling her.

At last Mr Arnold spoke. "Don't cry. I've been telling you you're such a special girl from the very first time you came into The Raven's Nest. You're the girl who will live forever in The Midnight House."

"Please," said Clarabelle. "I want to go home now."

At first, her voice was a whisper, but she thought about her mum and Tobias. She also thought about Thomas, Iris, Petra and Arthur, her wonderful neighbours. She felt courage swell in her heart. The dolls had tricked her all this time to trap her in the house! She'd finally let them in: she thought they were her friends, her best friends, and it was all a lie. Her fear turned to anger. She stomped her foot on the floor for good measure. The dolls circled Clarabelle, drawing even closer to her. She could even smell their musty clothes.

"Home?" barked Merlin. "This is your home now. You were lucky Papa sold your mum The Midnight House at half price. You're special. The last girl didn't work out, but you will. You did so well guarding the snow globe all this time, you showed your loyalty to us."

This can't be happening, thought Clarabelle. She couldn't allow herself to think about the last girl and what happened to her. She had to get out of

The Midnight House. She needed to get back to Mum.

Mr Arnold ambled over to the window and pulled back the white silk curtains. "You see, Clarabelle," he said. "Your old life is slipping further and further away. You'll have a wonderful life with us."

Mr Arnold nodded, and the dolls broke the circle. Clarabelle peeked out of the window and saw her bedroom far away, like she was in the sky, looking down at it. It would soon be out of sight.

The dolls' eyes now had a white sheen. They began to glow brighter than the moon. The doll's house became cold. The fire died.

"I want my mum," Clarabelle cried.

"Your mum bought you The Midnight House. Mums know best," said Mr Arnold. "She would want a good life for you, a better life. Remember you're the girl who wanted The Midnight House so much your teeth hurt, you were dizzy, you couldn't sleep, you got brain freeze. Do you think I didn't notice you staring in the window of my shop every weekend?"

"Only because I thought it was beautiful. But I don't think it's beautiful any more," Clarabelle told him.

Evie and Merlin started to cry. "Mama and Papa, she must stay. The Midnight House is no good without Clarabelle Graves. We love her like a sister and a best friend. We're lonely," they chirped in unison.

"I have a mum and my best friend, Tobias. And I love school," Clarabelle said.

"Tobias doesn't care about you any more. And your mother has plenty of friends. You have to stay," said Merlin.

"Yes!" said Evie. "You've had plenty of time with your mother and friends. Mama is better than all the teachers in the world. We need you."

"It's past your bedtime. You'll go to sleep in your new bedroom," Mr Arnold said. "And once you sleep there, you'll be here forever in

The Midnight House."

Clarabelle remembered her mum's words: "Stand up for yourself, Clarabelle Graves!" She screamed so loud she thought her lungs would burst. Maybe if she screamed loud enough, her mum would hear her. "Mum, Mum, Mum!" she cried.

But it wasn't her mum who answered.

"Clarabelle? Clarabelle? Is that you? Where are you? I can hear you whispering. You seem so far away."

Through the window, Clarabelle saw a shadow fall across her faraway bedroom. A familiar shadow. One she knew as well as her own. "Tobias!" she screamed.

Tobias stopped. He stood in Clarabelle's bedroom like a giant, towering over The Midnight House. "Clarabelle? Where are you? I can barely hear you. Your mum let me in. I was worried about you."

Tobias bent down and looked under Clarabelle's bed and peered into the closet. Clarabelle saw his face wrinkled with worry.

"Tobias!" she screamed again. "I'm in here. I'm trapped in the doll's house." Clarabelle pressed her face against the window, she banged on the glass, but it felt like stone.

"He can't hear you," hissed Merlin. "You're in The Midnight House, remember? Why are you calling to that boy?"

"Yes, Clarabelle, why are you?" said Evie. "That boy is more interested in rabbits. Dolls will love you forever. And we are forever dolls. Tobias isn't your friend any more. You haven't been to his house in weeks. What happened to Saturday film nights?"

Mr Arnold and Clarice laughed. Then Merlin joined in. They laughed so hard that Clarabelle thought all of the fine china and glassware would shatter in The Midnight House.

"You lied to me," shouted Clarabelle. "You're not my friends. You were never my real friends!"

"Of course we are," said Evie. "We're your only friends, and soon we'll be your family. Forget about your mum and Tobias. We are all you need."

"No! I need my mum and my best friend!"

Mr Arnold sighed as he took the watch with the long silver chain from his waistcoat. "Enough of this prattle. It's bedtime for Clarabelle. It's time to go upstairs and sleep. The other dolls are waiting."

Evie and Merlin seized Clarabelle's arms and began to drag her from the window.

"Very soon, my children," Mr Arnold whispered.

"That's good, Papa," they chimed. Merlin tugged

Clarabelle's hair and laughed.

"You're all just wicked dolls," cried Clarabelle. "Tobias is my friend. You just want to keep me here like a doll, not a real friend."

As Evie and Merlin tightened their grip, Clarabelle wondered if she would ever see her mum again, if she would ever be back in her bedroom, if she would ever go to Tobias's family bakery. Her old life flashed before her like a film. She needed to get Tobias's attention.

"Clarabelle! Clarabelle!" She heard the friendly and familiar voice of Tobias calling out for her as his face filled the window of The Midnight House.

"He's looking in," shouted Clarice.

"Don't worry, my dear, he can't see us," said Mr Arnold.

Tobias began to tap on the glass. It was a soft tap, but inside The Midnight House, it felt like an earthquake. The house shook so violently that Evie and Merlin let go of Clarabelle. Evie pulled at Clarabelle's dress and the snow globe fell to the floor. The snow globe! At last Clarabelle saw her chance. She shoved the dolls away and reached for the snow globe. She grabbed it and stood up.

"Tobias! Tobias!" she cried.

For the first time, Clarabelle saw fear darken Mr Arnold's face. The dolls stared at her with dagger eyes, and Evie lunged towards Clarabelle. But Clarabelle raised the snow globe over her head and smiled, before she threw it on the floor with all her might and watched it smash into a thousand pieces.

"Clarabelle!" Tobias's voice boomed through the window, shattering the glass. "It's you! I can see you."

Tobias thrust his hand through the window jagged with broken glass. He gently scooped up Clarabelle like she was a little doll. Clarabelle looked at Mr Arnold, Clarice, Merlin and Evie. They just stood there, their mouths open in a silent scream. The broken snow globe oozed water and fake snow around their feet. The miniature Midnight House began to break apart. At the same time the real Midnight House began to splinter. Cracks sprouted across the walls and slates broke and fell.

"Tobias," pleaded Clarabelle. "Get me out of here!" She closed her eyes and hoped she would wake up in her own bed.

Chapter 12

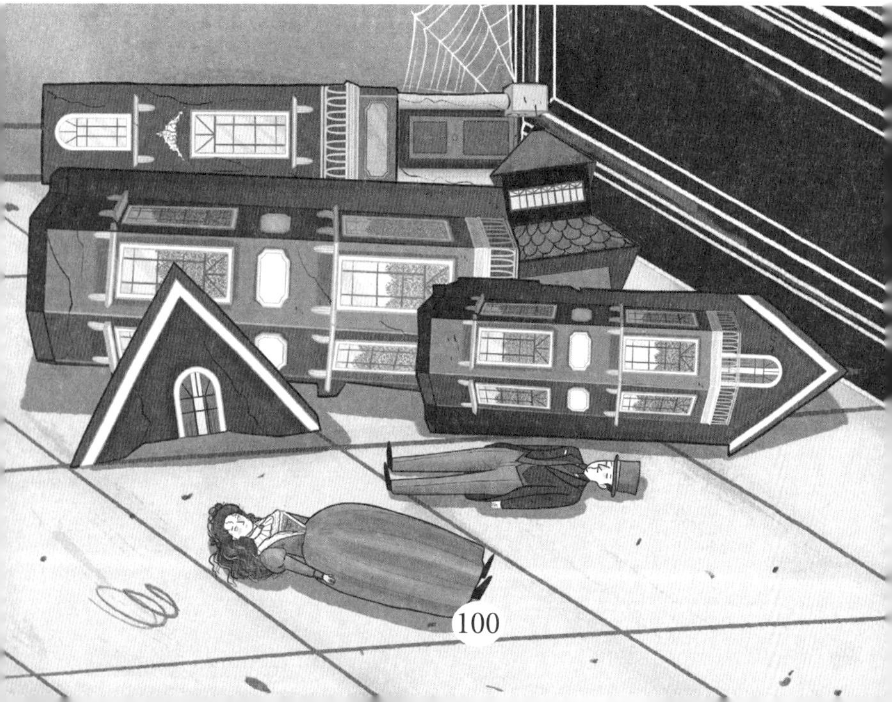

A few days later, Clarabelle stood outside the shuttered vintage shop with Tobias. There was a metal *For Sale* sign swinging from a rusty chain above the cracked front window. The door to the shop was chained shut and parts of the window were shuttered with splintery planks of rotten wood.

Clarabelle and Tobias peered through the gaps in the planks. They dared not say a word. They saw The Midnight House lying on its side in an ocean of dust. It was broken apart like an unwanted jigsaw puzzle. A doll like Mr Arnold with the same top hat lay on the floor with its eyes closed. Beside it was Clarice. Her gold gown was full of cobwebs. There was no sign of the old dinner sets, the antique

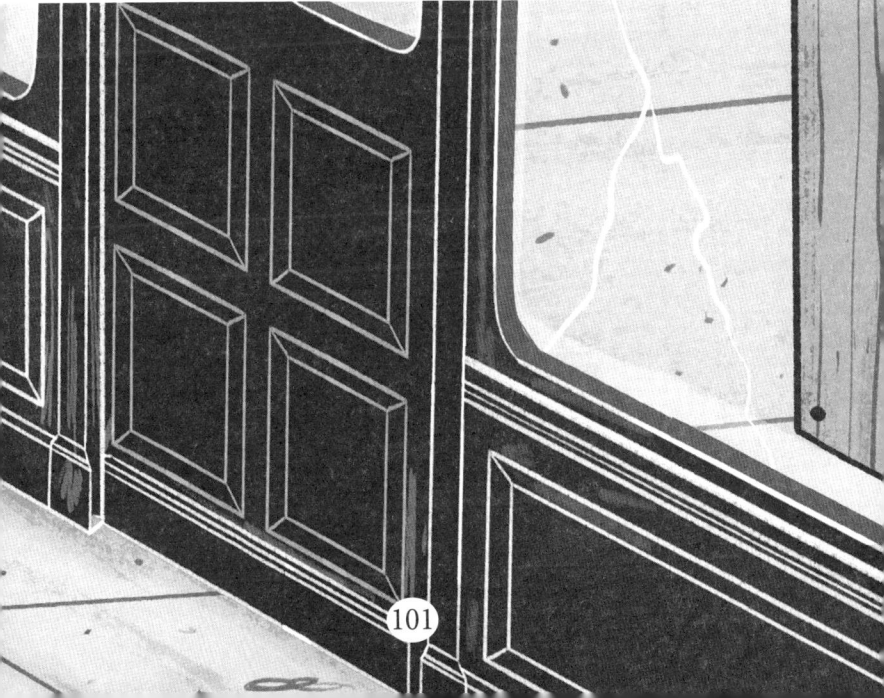

vases, the stuffed fox or the spinning wheel.

Clarabelle felt a thunderstorm in her heart and looked deeper through the window. She glimpsed Evie's satin shoe sticking out of a drawer. She went on tiptoes and saw Evie clearly lying on a dusty rag with Merlin. They were motionless, their eyes closed. Their hair looked grey, and their faces had lost the rosy glow.

"Did this really happen?" whispered Clarabelle. "I'm afraid to pinch myself again."

"How could we have both imagined it?" asked Tobias.

"Maybe I'm dreaming now," replied Clarabelle.

Clarabelle clutched Tobias's hand. "I'm glad you're here," she said. "I haven't been a good friend. I wanted The Midnight House so badly."

Tobias looked down at his feet and kicked some gravel on the pavement. Together, they'd moved the broken doll's house out of Clarabelle's bedroom and brought it over to the shop. The Raven's Nest already looked as though it had closed down a long time ago.

But the front door was open, so they just put the doll's house on the floor and got out as fast as they could. They hadn't said a word to each other until this moment.

Clarabelle was relieved that her mum didn't ask any questions and just said she was disappointed that the doll's house had fallen apart.

Clarabelle wasn't sure if Tobias would ever forgive her for choosing The Midnight House over their friendship. But then he smiled and said, "Hey, Clarabelle, don't you know what day it is?"

Clarabelle thought for a moment, trying to break through the brain fog. "No," she laughed. "After everything that's happened, I don't!"

"It's Saturday! That means it's film night."

Clarabelle smiled too and let the warm feeling wash over her. It was a great feeling. The type of feeling that you only get from a true friend.

They heard a flutter on the roof. A raven did a *pruk* sound. It was like the bird with the hooked bill was saying, "*This is over.*"

Clarabelle stole one last look at the dolls. The Midnight House's magic was gone forever.

Book talk questions

What makes Clarabelle such a relatable character?

How do the creepy dolls represent Clarabelle's fears and challenges?

What does Clarabelle learn about herself throughout the story?

How do the magic and mystery of the doll's house affect the atmosphere of the book?

How would you have reacted if you were in Clarabelle's shoes, trapped in the doll's house?

What role does Clarabelle's bravery play in her escape from the doll's house?

Why do you think the dolls want to keep Clarabelle in the magical world?

What does Clarabelle's struggle to return home teach us about resilience?

What toy would you like to come to life? What do you think would happen?

What do you think will happen next for Clarabelle and her friends now that The Midnight House is gone?

Ask the author

How did you start writing?

Eibhlís Carcione

I've always loved books and stories, especially spooky stories on stormy nights. I loved stories so much I began to write. When I was in secondary school, I realised there was something to my writing when a teacher thought a grown-up had written my story. When I was studying to be a teacher my writing was encouraged, and my first poems and stories were published.

What do you enjoy about writing?

I love everything about writing. It's the closest thing to magic. Words are very powerful and help fuel my imagination. I'm also bilingual and write in Irish. It's an ancient and mysterious language with a well of different words for many things, including doll.

Do you have a favourite place to write?

I write at a small antique desk in my front room, overlooking the crab apple tree in my garden. My two dogs are usually at my feet.

If you could live in any book world, which one would it be?

It would have to be *The Lion, the Witch and the Wardrobe* by C.S. Lewis. I would love to be Lucy's friend and to go through the wardrobe into Narnia.

If you could be one of your characters for a day, who would you choose and why?

I would love to be Clarabelle because she's plucky and inquisitive and it would be cool to go into The Midnight House but not for long!

What do you want readers to learn from Clarabelle's adventure?

Wanting something too much may not be a good thing. Be careful what you wish for!

Why did you choose dolls as the magical characters in the story?

My daughter collects vintage dolls and has a lovely collection in her room. One day when I went into her room one of the dolls fell off the shelf. I stared into the doll's eyes and knew I wanted to write a story about magical dolls.

Published by Collins
An imprint of HarperCollins*Publishers*

The News Building
1 London Bridge Street
London SE1 9GF
UK

Macken House
39/40 Mayor Street Upper
Dublin 1
D01 C9W8
Ireland

Text © Eibhlís Carcione 2025
Illustrations and design © HarperCollins*Publishers* Limited 2025

10 9 8 7 6 5 4 3 2 1

ISBN 978-0-00-874486-1

All rights reserved. No part of this publication may be reproduced, stored in a retrieval system, or transmitted in any form by any means, electronic, mechanical, photocopying, recording or otherwise, without the prior written permission of the Publisher or a licence permitting restricted copying in the United Kingdom issued by the Copyright Licensing Agency Ltd, 5th Floor, Shackleton House, 4 Battle Bridge Lane, London SE1 2HX.

Without limiting the author's and publisher's exclusive rights, any unauthorised use of this publication to train generative artificial intelligence (AI) technologies is expressly prohibited. HarperCollins also exercise their rights under Article 4(3) of the Digital Single Market Directive 2019/790 and expressly reserve this publication from the text and data mining exception.

British Library Cataloguing-in-Publication Data
A catalogue record for this publication is available from the British Library.

Author: Eibhlís Carcione
Illustrator: Beatriz Castro (Advocate Art)
Publisher: Laura White
Commissioning editor: Holly Woolnough
Development editor: Zoë Clarke
Product manager: Holly Woolnough
Content editor: Selin Akca
Copyeditor: Sally Byford
Proofreader: Catherine Dakin
Reviewer: Lisa Davis
Cover designer: Sarah Finan
Internal design: 2Hoots Publishing Services Ltd
Typesetter: Jouve India Ltd
Production controller: Katharine Willard

Collins would like to thank the teachers and children at Grange Primary School, Southwark, for being part of the development of Big Cat Read On.

Printed in the UK.

MIX
Paper | Supporting responsible forestry
FSC™ C007454

This book contains FSC™ certified paper and other controlled sources to ensure responsible forest management.

For more information visit: www.harpercollins.co.uk/green

Made with responsibly sourced paper and vegetable ink

Scan to see how we are reducing our environmental impact.

Get the latest Collins Big Cat news at
collins.co.uk/collinsbigcat